Tiffany and I

A not-so-romantic poetic comedy

Michalis Ghalanos

ISBN 979-8562294234

With gratitude,

Editing and blurb by Tell Tell Poetry
Cover illustrations by Enzo Triolo
Graphic design by Andrea Delbene
Interior design by Ekow Addai

Tiffany and I

Contents

Part 1

Meeting Tiffany

First day in an economics class

and I'm already wishing for a grade to pass.

The lecturer looks cold and unapproachable,

while the exercises seem practically unsolvable.

A girl in front of me grabs my attention—

her majestic hair compels my admiration.

Burning with curiosity, I lean over to ask her name.

She whispers, *It's Tiffany*, and my heart goes astray.

Her face is sculpted in perfect orthogonials—

her lips and eyes synthesizing a smoothing polynomial.

I tell her, *Hi*, and, *My name is Tom*.

She looks like a Queen, but I'm a humble pawn.

Her nose is lifted up and commands me to abstain.

You are quite cute, but your style is a pain.

Either you'll dress up properly for a girl of my posh

or stay away from me. Just simply: get lost!

Her words were certain—cruel but deliberate—

as her standard was too high and stiff to negotiate.

Yet I will surpass her imposed red lines,

even if I have to try numerous times,

and become the elegant King in her life.

Part 2

Awe and Reflection

End of class and I am still amazed

by Tiffany's looks and excessive haste

with putting forward her standards for a boyfriend,

as if inviting me not to disappoint her

and to look debonair for a lady of her class,

carrying myself with finesse whenever I enter class.

Economics deadlines may be looming,

but in my mind there's only grooving

to take her downtown, either to Swanky Joe's

or to the lounge bar by the Mermaids' shore.

The latter though might be too romantic

and risk surprising her into acting frantic.

So I will have to show a touch of gentle reservation,

unless I'd rather spend my night with econometrics estimations.

I will have to show character and approach her for this date,

as it is clearly written in our common fate

to be together for at least one night

and manifest memories that last for life.

The problem is, how am I going to ask her out

without being rejected and feeling an empty cloud?

I could say that every time I see her

I feel like dolphins dancing in a river

with heart-shaped shells and romantic little waves

peacefully ambling across a sunset-coloured mountain range

and gracefully falling at its edge over a valley of light-blue roses

that abundantly provides for pairs of love-struck wild horses.

Alas, those things are more than obvious to her

and she probably hears it every day without any rest,

that she's pretty enough to attract any guy with a blink.

Why don't you date me? There's nothing more to dream.

I wonder if someone has ever challenged her domains—

stimulating her intellect and not offering praise.

Would it be possible to tingle her curiosity

by treating everyone with gregarious generosity?

But all I know is that time is running by

and my chances will inevitably subside

if I don't make a move right now

in some direction. But, please, do tell me how

I'll find the courage to reapproach her

before someone else comes to her closer

and mesmerises her heart away from mine.

Part 3

A First Course in Dating

An act of courage to laud

was to—finally—propose to Tiffany, *Let's go out!*

I approached her with confidence and poise

and she accepted, but with a choice:

Either you're gonna take me to a chic place in town

or you'll rent a DVD and stay home like a clown.

I had no incentive to decline

as her luminous presence brings paradise to life.

So I took her down to Swanky Joe's

for decadent sambuca and tequila shots.

She was wearing a stunning black dress

that was begging to be touched and caressed.

I found the guts to stroke her hair

as my hunting flair was laying bare.

She placed her right hand on my left knee,

inviting me to further proceed.

My eyes were magnetised by her charming face

and I could have stared at her for endless days.

I crawled my fingers to her right cheek

and she started blushing as I heard her speak,

Come and sit closer to me, Tom,

'cause I'm mesmerised by your manly tone.

Her voice was gentle and delightfully exciting

as I started to feel something suddenly arising.

She touched my face in a slow, certain move

and leaned forward with a dazzling, sexy look.

Her lips were inviting me to make a pass,

but, unfortunately, I had a lot of gas.

I couldn't help but to eventually fart

and I actually shitted my Armani pants.

She started screaming and jumping up and down

and she spilled tequila all over her expensive gown.

I was mortified and said to her, *I'm sorry.*

And she thundered at me, *Get lost, you village boy!*

I watched her racing towards the exit

as I reflected on my lonely bedsit

that I was going to be alone.

Part 4

The Day After

On the following day, while cleaning my expensive dress,

my cell phone beeped—I had an SMS.

It was from that filthy idiot, Tom,

who blasted his underwear like an atomic bomb.

He said he was sorry and wanted to make things up

by taking me for an evening cruise into the setting sun.

I was prompt to decline—not because of fear of drowning,

but because it was dry and gators might be crawling.

On top of that there might not have been enough toilets on board

and what would happen if he let out another bomb?!

But he was persistent and insisted on taking me out

by offering dinner at a classy restaurant in town.

I was sceptical but, in the end, I accepted

in the hope that first impressions could be eventually amended.

And so, Tom drove by at around eight o'clock

and I could hear the barking of the neighbour's dog.

He told me, *Hi,* and, *Come on in,*

while giving an asymmetric grin.

I smiled back and got into the car.

We drove off for town, speeding into the dark.

The lights were subdued. The music was gentle and romantic

and behind the emerging waiter was a couple, intimately dancing.

I ordered spicy beef with a mixture of topical herbs,

while Tom requested a salad wearing a vinaigrette dress.

The waiter asked us what we would like to drink

and I said, *A glass of Chilean chardonnay*, without a blink.

Tom would just have a glass of sparkling water.

He was drinking light, afraid his stomach might groan, *Game Over*.

We talked about hobbies, travelling, and fashion—

kept it light-hearted, without lust or passion.

At one point, he asked inquisitively about my dreams in life

and challenged me to pursue them with determination and pride.

I warned him, *Don't be stupid*—but my heart was his

for his manly looks and intellectual tease.

He boldly leaned over, approaching my face,

softly whispering that I have a *hot* taste.

He tried to kiss me with immense desire

but I held back to set him on fire.

Very well, he said with a perky smile.

Why don't we go to my place and watch The Green Mile?

That film's starring actor is Tom Hanks.

But my Tom is an even greater hunk,

so I said, *Yes*.

Part 5

Land of Rhodium

I woke up early in the morning

with a craving to go jogging.

Next to me lay a beautiful princess

still asleep and in complete recess.

Her skin was desirable; her lips were soft.

But I had given it a lot of thought

and decided not to wake her up

as there was still a deplorable damp.

Last night was a fantasy, a fairy's dream.

She is easily the most attractive girl this house has ever seen.

We watched Stephen King's outstanding *Green Mile*

while eating popcorn and drinking chamomile.

I put my arm around her shoulder

and she reacted by crossing her border.

Take me upstairs, she nodded.

I want to see your bedroom. A miracle unfolded.

I held her hand as we entered my room.

She stumbled on a game console I wish I had flushed down the loo.

I kicked it aside and heard a tiny *vroom*

and then there came a massive *BOOM!*

Tiff was startled but didn't panic—

she was laughing with the flaming plastic.

I picked up everything and threw it outside,

hoping that her fire would not subside.

Luckily, Tiffany did not mind at all—

she grabbed me tight and pushed me on the floor.

I was overcome by desire and quickly got up to my feet.

She was growling with hunger—they could hear us on the street.

I hastily unbuttoned her expensive dress

and she unzipped my trousers in a little less.

I thought of Superman and lifted her in the air,

then landed her on my bed with extensive care.

All of a sudden, her face changed—

she turned sour and I was amazed.

What's the matter? I was keen to enquire.

Your bedsheet's wet. Have you peed, my esquire?

I was astounded and could sense the sarcasm in her voice,

but I was more disturbed by the abrupt halting of our noise.

Still, I was stranded and had no words to reply,

as there came a thunder—storms were in excess supply.

Immediately, it began to rain vigorously outside,

but I could see droplets falling on my Aphrodite.

We both looked up to see the roof leaking;

and so, we spent the night trying to fix the ceiling.

At around four a.m., Tiffany was beginning to break down.

I could see she was exhausted and in need of cooling down.

I was about to bring her tea with cookies and a wafer,

but she collapsed on my bedsheet while I was boiling water.

I carried on working until around five,

when I started writing poetry, to seduce away the night.

The storm was still mighty and serving its rainfall duty,

but was insufficient to wake up my little beauty.

After listening for a bit to 1990s hip-hop,

I decided it was time to rock-a-bye Tom on the treetop.

So I lay beside my sleeping princess,

kissed her goodnight, and minded my own business

of resting till dawn.

Part 6

Introducing Robert Al-Sahar

I was chilling with my hunk at a high-class café,

having a cup of Earl Grey with a hint of chardonnay.

Today is such a glorious day, sunshine all around.

Unlike last night at Tom's, when his roof was breaking down.

Tom's phone buzzed; it was a call from his professor.

He was commanding him to come perfect his calibrations.

A deadline is a deadline, and so Tom got up to go.

He kissed me on the lips with a joyous, radiant glow.

I stayed a bit longer, gazing over nothing,

thinking of last night and how I found myself laughing

over Tom and his unparalleled talent for destruction,

despite trying everything to add charm to his clumsy actions.

Still, I find him rather sweet, and always sincere

in working for the best with his motives clean and clear.

Suddenly, my senseless staring stopped and I landed onto reality.

A man taking his seat across my table subjected my daydreams to gravity.

He was tall and handsome, with marked muscles and swimmers' shoulders;

and most importantly of all, he was dressed like Kenny Rogers.

I subconsciously exuded a suggestive grin.

He noticed and smiled back; he had perfect white teeth.

Within seconds he got up and slowly approached me.

He told me, *I desire you. I want your pretty face along mine.*

I was shocked by the certainty in the directness of his move.

He was confident and daring, and it was feeling damn good.

I coyly gave another smile and asked him for his name.

He told me, *It is Robert, but I'm Bob for silky dames.*

He grabbed my hand and took me to the nearby parking place.

He had a bike with an inscription: *Al-Sahar won this race.*

Gallantly, he asked me to join him for a ride.

He had a ranch with white horses close to the seaside.

I was inclined to decline; Tom would have been devastated.

But Bob's fragrance was Emporio and I was deludingly persuaded

to succumb to *yes.*

Part 7a

Tom's Dissertation

I will explain this model in simple terms

because *I like it* and it would make more sense.

Assume that a representative single guy enters a highly stylized market.

He's on the lookout for a mate and *(I'll insert here a closing bracket.*

His utility is monotonically increasing with the mated girl's quality,

as well as inversely with time taken to find love in harmony.

Begin with considering the diagram below

and be prepared for me to take a bow:

Diagram 1

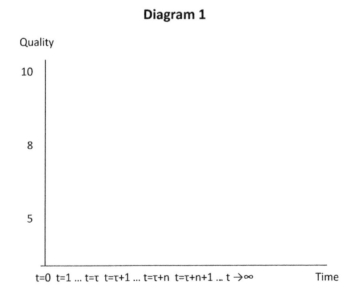

Quality

10

8

5

t=0 t=1 ... t=τ t=τ+1 ... t=τ+n t=τ+n+1 .. t →∞   Time

On the x-axis, I have "time"

from zero to infinity. *(I'm sorry, it doesn't rhyme!)*

On the y-axis, I have the "girl's subjective quality"

from zero to ten, with ten being surreality.

For ease of exposition, let's define this sweet number as "Tiffany"—

a clean ten out of ten, converging in the steady state to epiphany.

The next diagram portrays the agent's preference for "patience."

Please assume here that he has well-defined "tastes."

You could say that, by some law I don't quite remember,

the more he waits, the greater the chance of finding someone better.

So this line is trending upwards:

Diagram 2

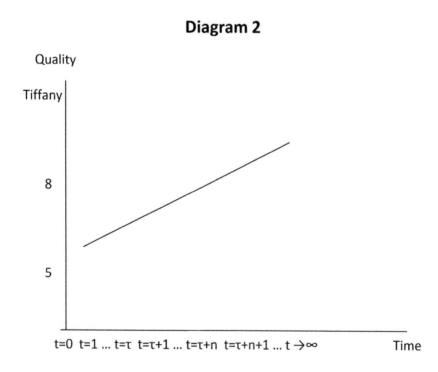

Consider now that the more this guy waits,

the more απηυδισμένος[1] he gets and really can't wait.

So if we are going to illustrate this in our simple and straightforward model,

we will have to envisage how much time it would take for him to falter and diminish down to his "desperation point":

Diagram 3

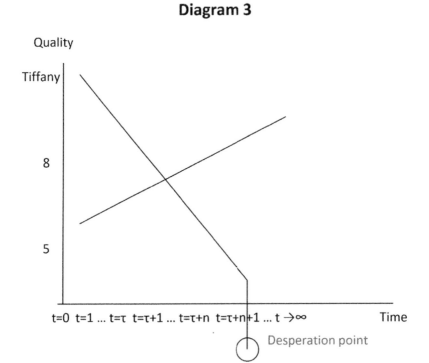

It is crystal clear that a unique and stable equilibrium exists— defined as the "bliss point"—and is attained in the medium term, it seems.

And this is how I close the model.

---

1   Translation: "frustrated, agitated, stupid man" (Swanky Joe's Concise Dictionary, 2007).

Thank you for reading, but please stay a bit longer

for I examine an array of extreme scenarios in the appendix

with graphs I did not have the time to create with Excel spreadsheets,

and neither with R.

Diagram 4

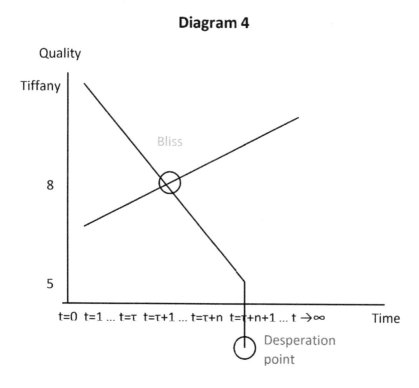

Appendix: Extreme Scenarios

CASE 1: Corner solution ("The George Clooney solution")

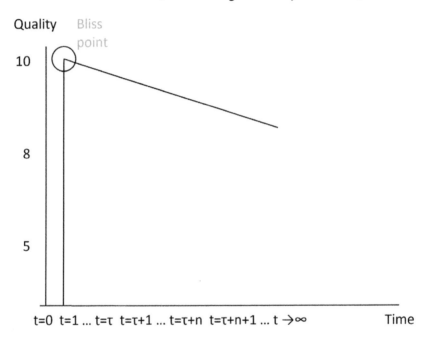

CASE 2: Loser-guy-who-stubbornly-refuses-to-lower-his-standards scenario ($\neg \exists$ sol^n)

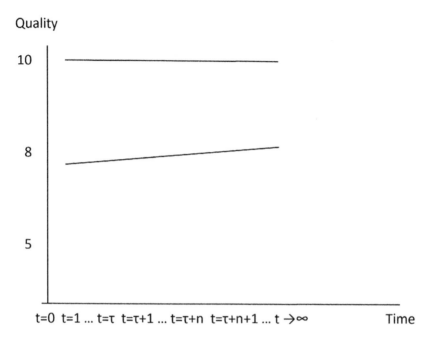

Part 7b

Re: Tom's Dissertation

I was reading Tom's economics dissertation,

which seems to be the best in many generations,

even though he made a few mistakes in various places.

He erroneously denoted the continuous stream of girls with the agent's

"patience,"

which girls, I reckon, are implicitly assumed to be single and attracted

to him,

because otherwise it would be a model of unbenevolent dictatorship.

Not to mention that he forgot to verify and insert a bracket at the beginning,

I am also doubtful about the sources he used to translate the agent's

unfulfillment.

It is disappointing he did not mention possible extensions.

He could have considered states of multiple equilibria in real-life

applications.

There could be a possibility of segregated markets and one girlfriend in

each.

Or he could change religion and make it moral to have three.

Nevertheless, I will give him an A because *I like it.*

It is a model with insight that adds to the profession's variety.

Tom also appears to be a decent guy; he works very hard,

despite obsessing over some girl. It's a shame he has no chance.

But this is economics we are dealing with and it is notoriously demanding.

He has to move on and focus on developing his academic standing,

if he wants one day to become a great economist. Like me.

Signed,

Professor Matthias von Öring

Part 8

Al-Sahar's Ranch

We were riding easy on the highway,

admiring the God-blessed landscape and wildlife.

We were breathing in the majestic, fresh air,

until a truck surpassed us, engulfing us in a toxic snare.

Pretty Tiffany was inevitably coughing on my shoulders.

It felt like bursts of breezes massaging me in forces.

We eventually took a detour to a bumpy country road.

It smelled a bit of manure and there was an intense glow

stemming from the sea's reflection of the dying sun in our eyes.

We were almost there. How quickly time flies!

Tiffany stepped down to joyously embrace the white horses.

In chess, like my friend Cherry, I'd sacrifice everything to retain my horses.

I held Tiffany's hand and walked her to the blackwood ranch house.

We had cuddling for *entrata* and sweetly lay on the real unicorn leather couch.

Gently, I poured onto Tiffany's eyes the soothing darkness of my palms.

And slowly, I strolled my fingers to her lips until she was completely calm.

Reject all judgment in this moment, I whispered to her mesmerised eyes.

And immerse yourself in lust until an unwilling sun ascends and shines.

Subtle tears started flowing from her eyes.

She looked up at me with a subdued smile.

I have to go back to Tom, she announced.

Part 9

Hausaufgabe

It is four a.m. and I am still struggling with metrics.

Oh dear Lord, this is tougher than advanced Tetris.

Those von Öring assignments are simply unbeatable to me.

How is it possible to regress 1970s inflation and get stationarity?

I can only think of experimenting with residual serendipity

that would magically eradicate those jumps, albeit nonintuitively.

But hang on a second! I think I've just come up with a profound idea

that has the potential to alleviate my forward-expected sleep apnoea.

I could consider utilising an array of Tiffany-type dummies to seductively

remove the plethora of outliers

and immerse sunshine on my regression's diagnostics for correlation,

normality, and heteroskedastic white-noise barriers.

Then my inflation variable would become $I(0)$ and fit for estimation

and nail yet another A-star to frame for inspiration.

That would make mom and papa proud :-)

Suddenly a pair of intense bright lights illuminates my apartment.

Is it God pouring His warm light to convey His holy Gladness?

I feel as if a powerful white rainbow is shining on my essence.

I can even hear an angel singing my name at the entrance.

Oh dear Lord, has the time finally arrived

that my seminal homework answers will be carved in the profession's
archives?

Yes, my Lord! I'm ready to spread my wings and become the great economist I was destined to be!

The time has come to fulfil the prophecy; we live in unprecedented times
indeed!

I've been preparing so long for this moment, dear sweet Lord! I'm finally
ready to bestow myself on our eternal quest for knowledge and breathtaking
research that would knock on academic freedom's door!

TOM!

It was Tiffany.

Part 10

Tiffany Returns

TOM!

TIFFANY!

Oh, there you are. I forgot my cashmere-woven sanitary pads.

There you go.

Thanks! Good-bye!

Bye.

Confused and Dumbfounded Tom

I cannot accept this, Professor von Öring.

My heart is pounding for her and she left me squalling.

She has been my eclectic inspiration,

notwithstanding the agonizing perspiration

of dressing up to her stratospheric standards

and acting like a fiery, macho badass.

Tom, I summoned you to discuss your dissertation.

It is impressive, I must say. It conveys your dedication

to preparing essays of adequately high quality

and I enjoyed examining your "Tiffany" surreality.

Thus, I am delighted to mark this with an A.

Still, you need to sort yourself out and stand up straight.

You would do well to reinstate your focus in your life.

You are not the first to date a woman who made a man cry,

so do not get fixated and lose your potential.

There is a plethora of Tiffanies who are single out there.

You should keep evolving your capacity in economics.

You have the talent to shine and graduate with unfettered glory.

But don't dim your vision, Tom boy.

Part 12

Best Reluctant Friends Forever

As we were trekking through the park,

I was conscious of the nearing dark.

In view of us geniuses forgetting to bring our flashlights,

and with no moon lurking in the sidelines,

impalpable dangers could rise to the surface

to trip us over to land on our faces,

leaving our belongings fully exposed

for vultures to grab in a second or so

and abandon us hurt and book-naked.

Tom was panting and lagging far behind,

beaten and humiliated after a series of tries

to fortify a rose-tinted love affair

by creating a tender, loving lair

that never really managed to materialise in full;

and I could sense him feeling exorbitantly cruel

for not winning me over and succumbing to Robert "Bob" Al-Sahar,

whose charisma is impeccable and his poise sweeping me afar

to treasured kingdoms in which I feel safe and loved.

Oh, Al-Sahar, please come and rescue me!

Grab my hand and carry me to your harbour's safety.

This extracurricular nightmare is testing my ability

to project my posh inner light to shine the way out of this calamity

and finally come home!

Part 13

Chess Games

Tiffany: 1. Tom: 0.

Tiffany's report:

=-=-=-=-=-=-=-=-=

It was obvious from the beginning

that our game was going to be thrilling,

as Tom raucously started with the legendary Alekhine Defence

and transitioned to the posh Dragon Variation of the Sicilian Defence.

I have to admit though, it was not as bewitching as our previous encounter,

when Tom set up a reverse Queen's Gambit hoping to score on the counter

by grabbing a central pawn of mine, albeit temporarily

exposing his neophyte philosophy and pompous play mentality

to sacrifice development that would result in complete calamity

for my poor, little (but always charming and sincere) Thomas.

It would have been peculiar to me if Tom had not expected

that I was going to decline his gambit, as I would be offended

to sell off the poshest pawn of my pawns—

that is, the one guarding my Queen at the front.

So to create surprise inflation, I accepted his gambit

and allowed myself some room to employ my army

to attack Tom's fundamental line of defences

and dominate with admirable elegance to knock Tom on the fences,

which was the only anticipated trait of my game style of play.

This time I enjoyed myself between the middle and endgame,

when I performed masterful moves to amplify Tom's pain

by deploying forces to a seemingly non-innocuous part of the board—

which successfully deceived fearful little Tom

into fixing his rooks and bishops in complete sclerosis for protection,

notwithstanding the fierce pawn-storm attack I discreetly launched for obliteration—

and swiftly trapped his little Napoleon around his cramped congregation,

which required only one white knight to mate,

like that model in ECON 3044: Industrial Organization.

Extraordinary and classy result!

Tom's report

=-=-=-=-=-=-=-=

Tiffany wore a tantalising dress with suggestive cleavage,

which seductively misaligned my focal point of attack/defence mechanisms.

So naturally, I lost. In chess.

Bad result, but highly enjoyable game!

Lunch at Tiffany's

Tiffany,

Remember the good old days when we used to stay up all night
working on endless projects and revising for exams at the college library?
I never before felt such excitement and sense of meaning. At that time,
we thought of deadlines and assessment grades as only something tiny
in life.
The joy of learning and digging deeper was never obstructed by those
mere details.
We were, back then, well aware of how unfulfilling society's zero-sum
game is.
We were immersing ourselves in the pure and innocent joy of academic
discovery,
thriving on our quest for awareness and evolved spirituality
that is earned through a deeper level of understanding.

So how would you feel about celebrating our ongoing adventure
with an organic mango-mambo salad at Mermaids' shore lounge bar
at, say, 13:31?

Tom,

I vividly remember all those nights at the college library,

when 99.99% of the time you were staring at me instead of focusing on writing

the plethora of essays and econometric projects we were required to submit

in order to have a chance of celebrating on graduation's eve

that we'd have a good set of results to get a decent job,

ideally not updating charts or estimating ARCH and GARCH.

But, as you know, life moves on and we should exit our illusion

since our years will now slowly converge to an overall conclusion

that there's more to life in this world than a posh mango-mambo salad

or ultra-defensive chess games, as if you can never feel hurried up.

So it breaks my heart to disappoint you,

but I will firmly have to warn you

that I no longer eat salads, leaves, plants, or anything else that is vegetarian,

as I now consider all these to be anti-posh and utterly barbarian,

ever since I set off to a new leafy start

with my new amore, Robert "Bob" Al-Sahar,

the handsome gardener of my idyllic life!

Part 15

Tom Reborn

It was not meant to be

that Tiffany's affair would last to infinity,

as Al-Sahar's interests moved on.

He essentially dumped her without much of a second thought.

Bob is now cruising with von Öring's research assistant Amber,

which, in my opinion, is the epitome of a colossal blunder,

as no sane male would pass over Tiffany the Goddess.

But thankfully for me, man can succumb to acts of madness.

I gave Tiffany a call the other day

and, the compassionate idiot that I am, offered to listen to her pain.

Tiffany could see through me and asked me to hang out tonight.

She wanted to have fun and had already hell-sent Al-Sahar with no bye-bye.

So I took her again to Swanky Joe's

to have the familiar sambuca and tequila shots.

Tiffany was an explosive sight that night.

She wore an apocalyptic red dress that shattered the jaws of standers-by.

She had dyed her lustrous hair black

and looked like a Spanish princess electrifying Santana's guitar.

She gave me a wild kiss without a blink

and even bit my upper lip.

She grabbed my arms and danced me outside

and hailed a cab to take us to the riverside.

Oh dear, I thought.

It's bitterly cold but she is super-hot.

There's not much to imagine about how this would unfold.

Part 16

Red-Hot Blues

Fate would have it, but I can define my own life

and torch everything that irks my unforgiving sight.

I was certain Tom would have given me a call

and offer his pitying sympathies to comfort me in my fall

as if I'm a little girl scared of being alone,

helplessly in need of soothing a trauma that was painfully raw.

I appreciate his intentions and he'd be the wrong man whose head to bite off.

There's a blazing volcano inside me that needs to explode its way on,

so I commanded him to take me out to an adequately posh place,

if there was any chance at all I'd be able to save face.

I held his hand and entered Swanky Joe's establishment.

It was filled with Toms who stared at me in berserk astoundment.

But I was in no mood to galvanise the paleo instincts of the boys in there.

So I grabbed my Tom to take him where his imagination wouldn't dare.

We boarded a taxi to a fancy, five-star hotel by the riverside.

It was slightly chilly but Tom was shivering like a fish stranded in an

ebbing tide.

I asked him, *What's the matter, my sweetheart? It's not as if we've never ventured in forbidden lands.*

Suddenly the righteous philosopher awoke in him.

He told me he does not want to be a rebound and yearns for meaning in his relationships.

So we took a detour and left Tom in his empty casa;

and I continued with the toned taxi driver to an audacious extravaganza, who, hell would have it, was also named . . . Tom.

Printed in Great Britain
by Amazon

55320520R00031